This igloo book belongs to:

....

igloobooks

Published in 2019
by Igloo Books Ltd
Cottage Farm
Sywell
NN6 0BJ
www.igloobooks.com

1219 003
6 8 10 12 11 9 7 5
ISBN 978-1-78197-626-5

Illustrated by Jo De Ruiter

Printed and manufactured in China

Little Ted's BIG ADVENTURE

JO DE RUITER

igloobooks

One morning, Little Ted woke up and saw the sky was grey.

"I know just what to do," he said, "I'll go on holiday."

Ted hurried off to clean his teeth and wash his sleepy face.

He grabbed his little squeaky duck and quickly packed his case.

Ted hopped onto a speedy jet that zoomed him off to Spain.

"I do prefer the beach," he said, "instead of all that rain."

He built a huge sandcastle, made of seaweed, shells and sand.

Then sang and danced all evening, with a cool flamenco band.

In France, Ted bought the biggest, yummy treat he'd ever seen,

Made with chocolate sauce and caramel and sticky, mint ice cream!

He climbed the Eiffel Tower all the way without a stop. Ted felt worn out when halfway up, but made it to the top.

In Italy, Ted ate some slippy pasta with his bread.

The pasta slithered through his fork and splattered Little Ted!

Ted hired a floating gondola
which carried him away.

He floated down the Venice streets,
while singing all the way.

In Egypt, Little Ted explored a dark and creepy tomb.

He saw a spooky mummy standing in the murky gloom!

In China, Ted walked on the Wall and leapt right off the side!

He landed on a panda bear who took him for a ride.

Then, afterward, he joined
the panda for a bite or two.
They lazed on bright, green jungle
leaves while munching on bamboo.

"I think Great Britain will
be next," decided Little Ted.
So, off he went to meet the queen
for tea with jam and bread.

That afternoon, Ted went to watch a football match for fun.

"Come on, you reds!" sang Little Ted. "Now, score another one!"

Ted travelled to Australia
and met a wallaby,
Who tucked Ted in its
little pouch and let
him ride for free.

They leapt over a crocodile
who opened up one eye.

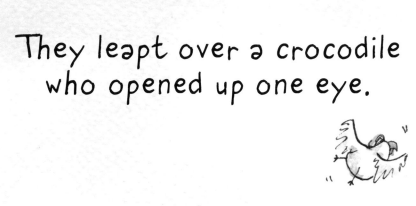

Its jaws went SNAP!
"Look out!" cried Ted,
as they went
bouncing by.

America was next. Ted said, "I've heard it's pretty good. I want to visit all the famous stars in Hollywood."

He boogied at a disco and he met a movie star,

Who whizzed him round a racetrack in his flashy racing car.

By now, poor Ted was feeling tired. "I'm quite worn out," he said. "I've loved my little holiday, but now I need my bed!"

"It's been a great adventure and I must come back one day." Ted packed his case and wearily he headed on his way.

At last, Ted reached his little
house and snuggled into bed.

"I've had a lot of fun, but now
I'm glad I'm home," he said.